PALM BEACH COUNTY
LIBRARY SYSTEM
3650 Summit Boulevard
West Palm Beach, FL   33406-4198

W9-BHJ-812

For Carmin, who inspired this series.
—KK

To my family, the glue to my glitter.
—GB

Henry Holt and Company, *Publishers since 1866*
Henry Holt® is a registered trademark of Macmillan Publishing Group, LLC.
120 Broadway, New York, New York 10271 • mackids.com

Text copyright © 2022 by Karen Kilpatrick.
Illustrations copyright © 2022 by Germán Blanco.
All rights reserved

Library of Congress Control Number: 2021047596
ISBN 978-1-250-81760-0

Our books may be purchased in bulk for promotional, educational, or business use.
Please contact your local bookseller or the Macmillan Corporate and Premium Sales Department
at (800) 221-7945 ext. 5442 or by e-mail at MacmillanSpecialMarkets@macmillan.com.

First Edition, 2022
Printed in China by RR Donnelley Asia Printing Solutions Ltd., Dongguan City, Guangdong Province

1 3 5 7 9 10 8 6 4 2

WHEN GLITTER MET GLUE

Story by Karen Kilpatrick

Illustrated by Germán Blanco

Henry Holt

New York

Once, there was a bottle of Glue

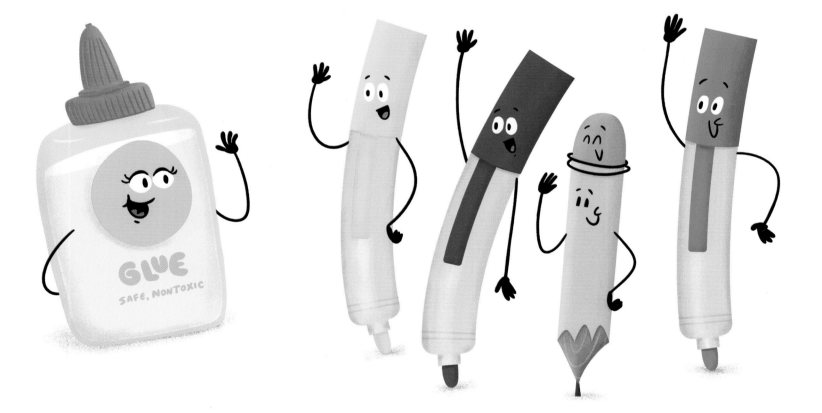

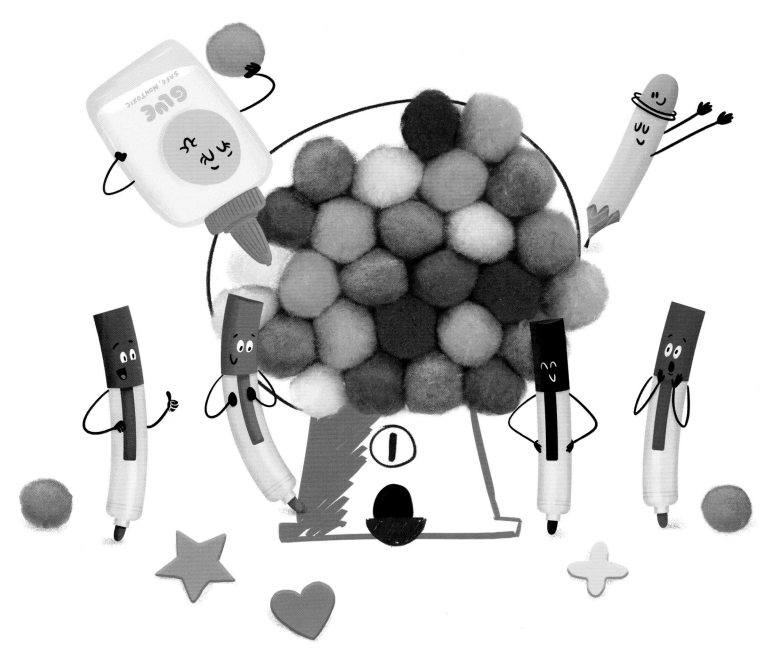

who liked to help her friends create art.

Glue made Popsicle sticks and pom-poms
stay in just the right place,

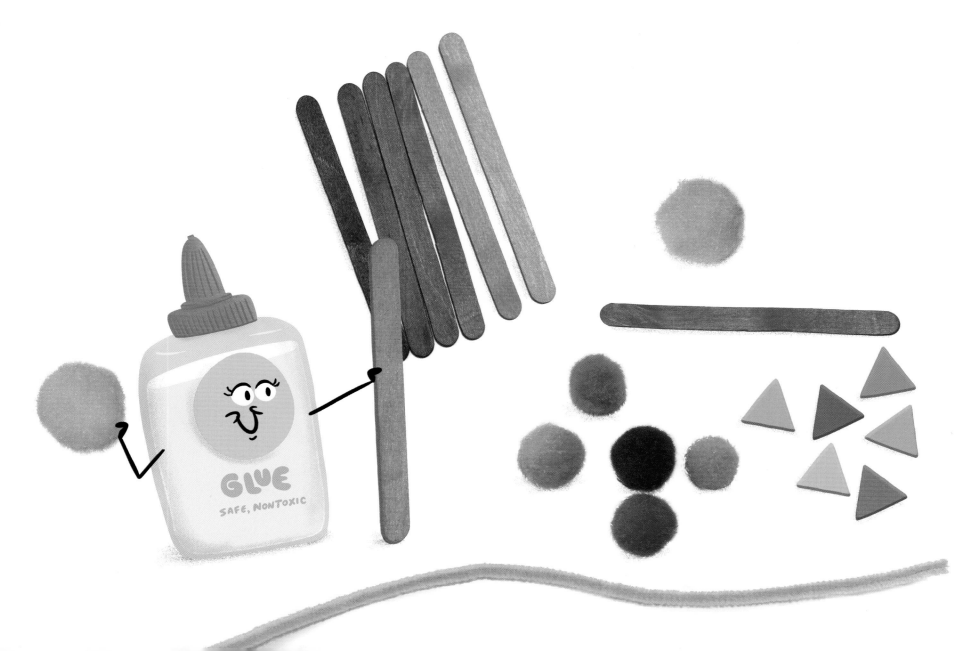

feathers and foam shapes stick to their spots . . .

and don't forget the googly eyes!

With Glue's help, anything was possible . . .

and anything could be turned into art!

But while Glue always poured her heart into her work, she felt a little low.

Glue wanted to be noticed like Pencil,
and to be colorful like the Markers!

Love the sprinkles, Markers!

That cone looks perfect, Pencil!

Even though Glue was useful, she was invisible.

Glue wondered if she'd always be stuck in the background, when something caught her eye . . .

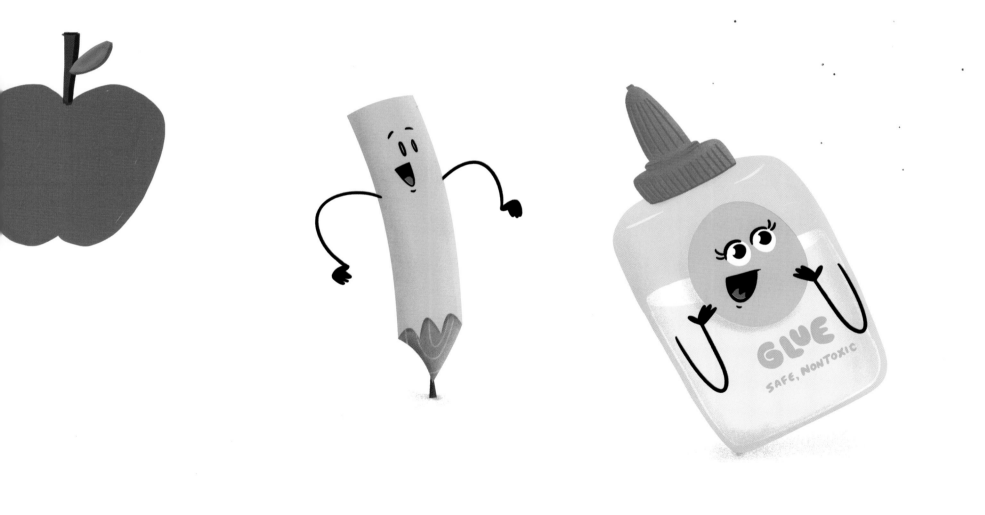

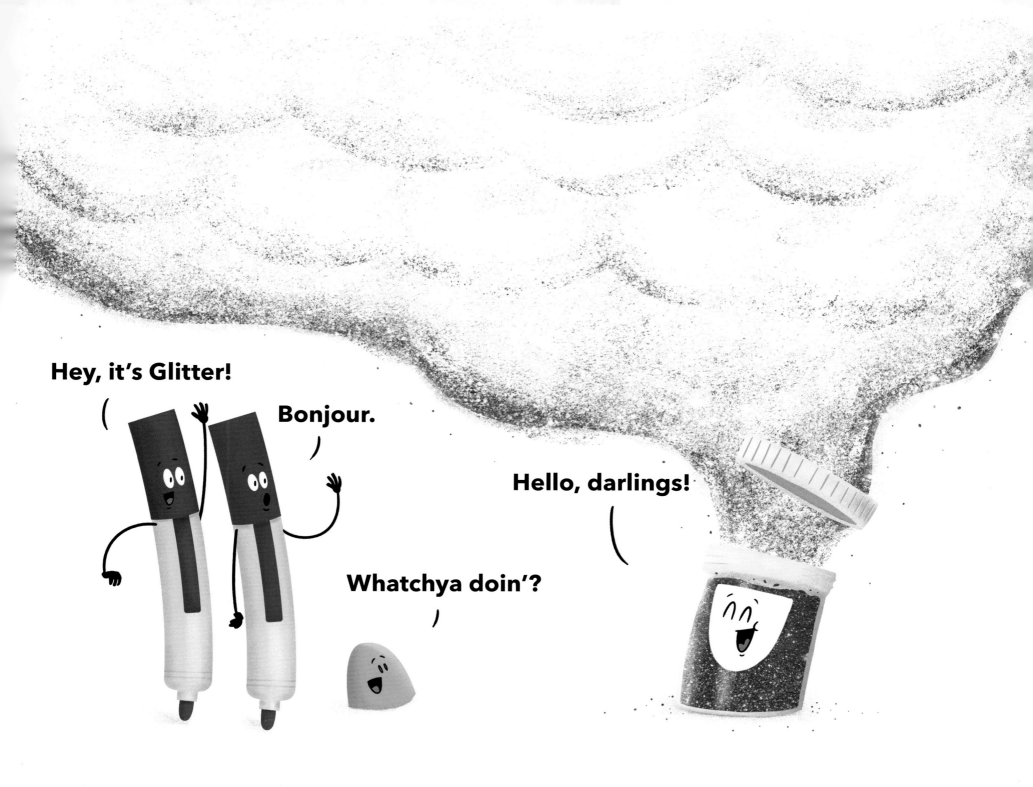

Glitter arrived in a swirl of sparkles, but Glue
noticed that they never stayed in one place.

**You know, I can make your
sparkles stick if you want . . .**

Glitter wasn't interested.

I was meant to sparkle the entire world, not just one tiny spot!

Glue had an idea. She carefully
poured a glob of glue for Glitter.

But Glue's glob nearly matched the color of the paper, and Glitter didn't see it. Glitter slipped, falling right into the glue!

Glitter's friends yanked and pulled,
and pulled and yanked until . . .

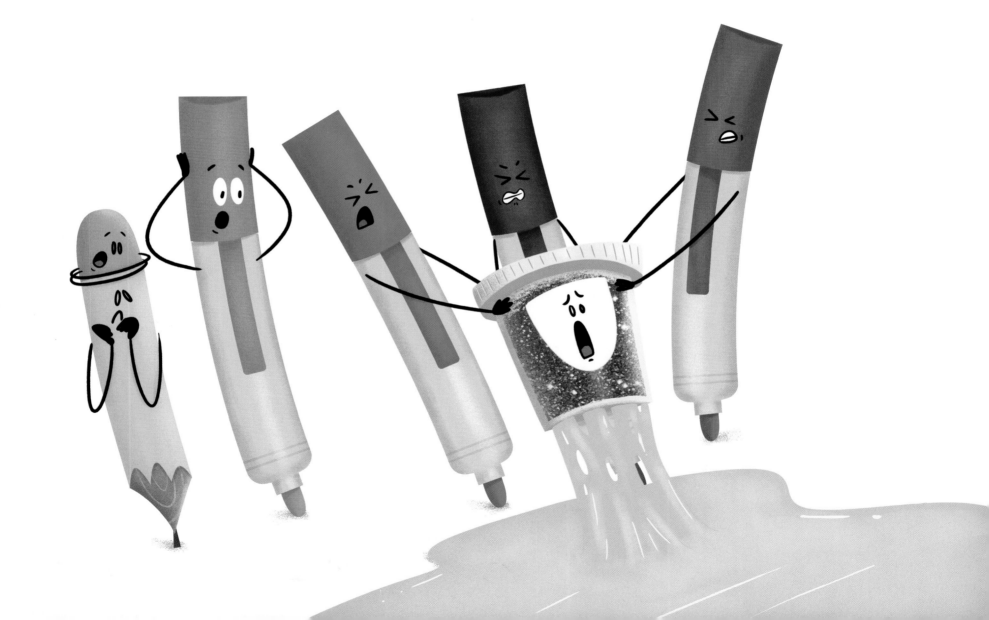

Glitter flew free and sparkles flew everywhere!

And there was glitter all over the glue!

How fabulous!

So Glue continued to glue, and Glitter continued to sparkle.

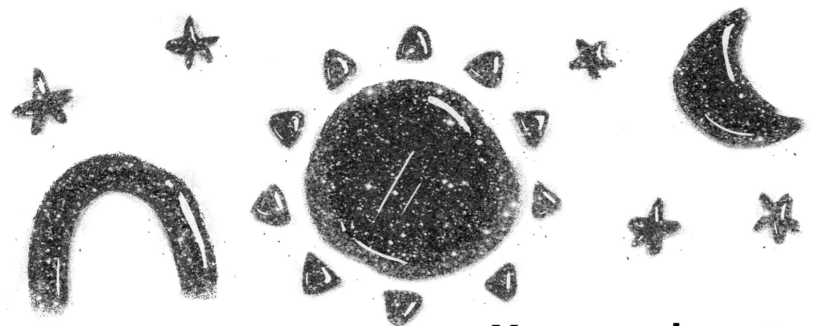

You were born to
SHINE,
darling!

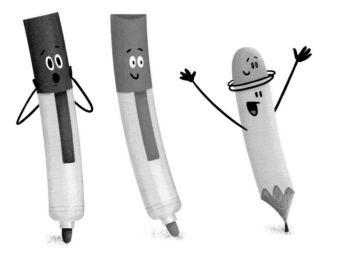

Glitter thought Glue was amazing and decided
to do something special for his new friend.

**So you can always be seen
for the star that you are!**

Glitter was now . . .